Dear Parent:
Your child's love of reading starts here!

Every child learns to read in a different way and at his or her own speed. Some go back and forth between reading levels and read favorite books again and again. Others read through each level in order. You can help your young reader improve and become more confident by encouraging his or her own interests and abilities. From books your child reads with you to the first books he or she reads alone, there are I Can Read Books for every stage of reading:

SHARED READING
Basic language, word repetition, and whimsical illustrations, ideal for sharing with your emergent reader

BEGINNING READING
Short sentences, familiar words, and simple concepts for children eager to read on their own

READING WITH HELP
Engaging stories, longer sentences, and language play for developing readers

READING ALONE
Complex plots, challenging vocabulary, and high-interest topics for the independent reader

ADVANCED READING
Short paragraphs, chapters, and exciting themes for the perfect bridge to chapter books

I Can Read Books have introduced children to the joy of reading since 1957. Featuring award-winning authors and illustrators and a fabulous cast of beloved characters, I Can Read Books set the standard for beginning readers.

A lifetime of discovery begins with the magical words **"I Can Read!"**

Visit www.icanread.com for information
on enriching your child's reading experience.

PONY SCOUTS

Really Riding!

For Tamar and Natalie
—C.H.

For Kathy, Moki, Laura,
and Mickey
—A.K.

HarperCollins®, ☙®, and I Can Read Book® are trademarks of HarperCollins Publishers.

Pony Scouts: Really Riding! Copyright © 2009 by HarperCollins Publishers All rights reserved. Manufactured in China. No part of this book may be used or reproduced in any manner whatsoever without written permission except in the case of brief quotations embodied in critical articles and reviews. For information address HarperCollins Children's Books, a division of HarperCollins Publishers, 10 East 53rd Street, New York, NY 10022. www.icanread.com

Library of Congress catalog card number: 2009920734
ISBN 978-0-06-125536-6
09 10 11 12 13 SCP 10 9 8 7 6 5 4 3 2 1

❖

First Edition

I Can Read!™

READING
2
WITH HELP

PONY SCOUTS

Really Riding!

by Catherine Hapka
pictures by Anne Kennedy

HarperCollins*Publishers*

Jill lived on a pony farm.
Today her two best friends
were coming home with her
on the school bus.

Jill, Meg, and Annie

called themselves the Pony Scouts.

They all loved ponies.

They loved hanging out together.

And they loved learning new things.

Today was a special day.

The Pony Scouts were sleeping over at Jill's house.

Meg and Annie were also having their very first riding lesson!

"Are you guys ready?" Jill asked.

"I can't wait!" Meg cried.

"I think I'm ready," Annie said.

She wasn't quite as brave

as Jill or Meg.

When they got to the barn
Jill's mom was waiting.
"Hello, girls," she said.
"Meg, you can ride Sparkle."

"Hooray!" Meg cheered.

She already loved Sparkle.

He was a spunky gray pony

who loved carrots.

"Annie, you can ride Splash,"
Jill's mom said.
Annie looked happy.
Splash was a gentle pinto pony.

Jill saw a chubby bay pony

watching them over her stall.

"Will anyone ride Rosy?" she asked.

Her mother shook her head.

"Rosy is brand-new on the farm.

It's too soon to ride her."

"Come on," Jill told her friends.

"I'll show you how

to get your ponies ready."

Jill showed Meg and Annie
how to brush the ponies
and clean their hooves.
Next she helped put on their tack.
"This is fun!" Meg said.

Then the lesson started.

Jill's mom was a good teacher.

Soon Meg and Annie

were riding their ponies

slowly around the ring.

"You guys are doing great!"
Jill said.
She took some pictures
with her mom's camera.

Meg and Annie learned how to move and how to stop.

Meg laughed out loud.

"I can't believe it!" she said.

I'm really riding!"

After the lesson

the girls stopped to pat Rosy.

"She's pretty," Annie said.

"Pretty fat, you mean!"

Meg said with a giggle.

Jill laughed, because it was true.

Rosy was a very round pony!

That night was the sleepover.
The Pony Scouts printed out
the photos Jill had taken that day.
"Tomorrow we can pin them up
on the bulletin board in the barn,"
Jill said.

"Cool," Annie said.

"The bulletin board can be
the Pony Scout headquarters!"

"Don't stay up too late, girls,"
Jill's mom said.
"In the morning you can
help me feed the ponies."

The girls talked and laughed.

They ate popcorn.

They were all wide awake,

even at midnight!

"Hey, I have an idea," Jill said.

"Let's sneak out to see the ponies!"

Sparkle was munching hay.

Splash was sleeping, but he woke up when Meg called him.

Annie walked over to Rosy's stall.

"Hey, you guys!" Annie said.

She sounded a little worried.

Jill hurried to see what was wrong.

She gasped at what she saw.

Rosy was standing there

beside a tiny, wobbly new foal!

"Oh my gosh!" Jill cried.

"We have to get Mom!"

They ran inside and told Jill's mom

about the foal.

Jill's mom was very surprised.

She called the vet right away.

He came a few minutes later

and checked Rosy and her baby.

"All is well," he said with a smile.

"Mom and foal are both healthy."

"Since you girls found the baby,

you can name him," Jill's mom said.

"I know!" Annie cried.

"We should name him Surprise!"

The friends all agreed.

It was the perfect name

for a perfect surprise foal!

PONY POINTERS

bay: A color of horse or pony that is mostly brown with black legs, mane, and tail

foal: A baby horse or pony

pinto: A spotted pony

tack: Another name for a saddle and bridle